Love & Tragedy
At
Pemberley

Love & Tragedy At Pemberley

1, Volume 1

Darryl Martel

Published by Darryl Martel, 2024.

LOVE & TRAGEDY AT PEMBERLEY

First edition. September 2, 2024.

Copyright © 2024 Darryl Martel.

ISBN: 979-8227744180

Written by Darryl Martel.

Also by Darryl Martel

Table of Contents

Prologue

It was Spring 1814, Elizabeth Bennet, now Mrs. Darcy, stood at the grand window of Pemberley, gazing out at the serene landscape that had become her home. The tranquil waters of the lake shimmered under the morning sun, and the lush greenery of the estate stretched out as far as the eye could see. Elizabeth felt a deep sense of contentment and gratitude for the life she now led with her beloved husband, Fitzwilliam Darcy.

It was a peaceful morning, yet there was a flutter of excitement in the air. Elizabeth had received a letter the previous week from an old childhood friend, Helen Baxter, whom she had not seen in years. Helen was to visit Pemberley and Elizabeth was eager to reunite with her, as the Baxter family had moved from Meryton some time ago. The two had. shared many happy memories during their younger days, and Elizabeth looked forward to rekindling their friendship.

Chapter 1
Friends

Helen Baxter had always been a lively and intelligent girl, with a quick wit and a kind heart. Elizabeth remembered their shared laughter, late-night conversations, and mutual support during challenging times. She wondered how time had treated Helen and what adventures and misadventures she had encountered since they last saw each other.

As Elizabeth turned away from the window, she heard the sound of footsteps approaching. She turned to see her husband, Fitzwilliam Darcy, entering the room. His presence always brought a smile to her face.

"Good morning, my dear," Darcy greeted her with a warm smile. "You seem deep in thought."

Good morning, Fitzwilliam," Elizabeth replied, walking over to him. "I was thinking about Helen Baxter. She should be arriving today, and I am quite eager to see her."

Darcy nodded, taking Elizabeth's hand in his. "I remember you speaking fondly of her. It will be a pleasure to meet her and welcome her to Pemberley."

Their conversation was interrupted by the sound of carriage wheels on the gravel path outside. Elizabeth's heart skipped a beat as she realised that Helen had arrived. She and Darcy made their way to the front entrance to greet their guest.

The carriage came to a halt, and the door opened to reveal a woman of about Elizabeth's age, with blonde hair and bright blue eyes. Helen Baxter stepped out, her face lighting up with joy as she saw Elizabeth.

"Elizabeth!" Helen exclaimed, rushing forward to embrace her friend. "It is so wonderful to see you!"

Elizabeth returned the embrace with equal enthusiasm. "Helen, it has been far too long! Welcome to Pemberley."

Helen stepped back, her eyes sparkling with excitement as she took in the grandeur of the estate. "Pemberley is even more beautiful than I imagined. You are truly fortunate, Elizabeth."

Elizabeth smiled, then turned to introduce her husband. "Helen, this is my husband, Fitzwilliam Darcy. Fitzwilliam, this is Miss Helen Baxter."

Darcy extended his hand in greeting. "It is a pleasure to meet you, Miss Baxter. Elizabeth has spoken very highly of you."

"The pleasure is mine, Mr. Darcy," Helen replied, shaking his hand. "I have heard much about you and I am delighted to finally meet you."

With the formalities complete, Elizabeth led Helen inside, where refreshments had been prepared. They spent the next hour catching up on each other's lives, sharing stories and laughter as if no time had passed since their childhood days.

Helen had traveled extensively since leaving school, experiencing the world, with her parents and all its wonders. She spoke of her adventures with enthusiasm, and Elizabeth found herself captivated by her friend's tales.

As the afternoon wore on, Helen's gaze wandered to the windows overlooking the gardens. "Pemberley is truly a paradise, Elizabeth. I can see why you love it here."

"It is indeed a wonderful place," Elizabeth agreed. "But it is the people who make it truly special. Fitzwilliam and I have found great happiness here."

Helen smiled warmly. "I am so happy for you, Elizabeth. You deserve every bit of happiness."

The next morning after breakfast, Helen and Elizabeth were discussing what they may do, as the sun was shining and Elizabeth, suggested a walk around the grounds. Helen's attention was drawn to a distant sound. She turned to Elizabeth with a curious expression.

"Elizabeth, who is that approaching?" Helen asked, nodding towards the window.

Elizabeth followed her gaze and saw a rider approaching on horseback. As the figure drew nearer, she recognised him as Lord James Percy, the youngest son of the Duke of Northumberland.

James was a frequent visitor to Pemberley, and he and Darcy shared a long-standing friendship.

"That is James, the son of the Duke of Northumberland," Elizabeth explained. "He often visits Pemberley, to see Fitzwilliam. I think you will find him quite charming."

Helen watched as James dismounted and handed his reins to a stable hand. He was a handsome young man, with dark hair and a confident manner. As he approached the house, Elizabeth and Helen made their way to the entrance to greet him.

James, welcome to Pemberley," Elizabeth said with a warm smile. "It is always a pleasure to see you."

James returned her smile. "Thank you, Elizabeth. It is good to be here." He then turned his attention to Helen, his gaze lingering on her for a moment longer than necessary. "And who is this lovely lady?"

"This is my dear friend, Miss Helen Baxter," Elizabeth introduced them. "Helen, this is Lord James Percy, the son of the Duke of Northumberland."

James bowed slightly. "It is a pleasure to meet you, Miss Baxter."

"The pleasure is mine, Lord Percy," Helen replied with a polite curtsey.

As they made their way back inside, Elizabeth couldn't help but notice the glances exchanged between Helen and James. There was a spark of interest in their eyes, a hint of something more than mere politeness. Elizabeth smiled to herself,

wondering if this unexpected visit might lead to something wonderful for her friend.

Fitzwilliam, greeted Lord Percy and they both went into Mr Darcy's study. Elizabeth and Helen, went to get ready for their walk.

An Evening at Pemberley

The evening at Pemberley was a lively affair, with guests gathered in the grand drawing-room, engaged in conversation and enjoying the warm hospitality of their hosts. Elizabeth and Darcy had invited a few close friends and neighbour's to join them in welcoming Helen, and the atmosphere was one of conviviality and merriment. Fitzwilliam's sister, Georgiana was herself, visiting her Aunt, so missed Helen's arrival, but once Georgiana returned, they had good conversation and Helen looked forward to hearing her play the pianoforte.

Helen, dressed in a lovely gown of pale blue, moved gracefully among the guests, her charm and wit endearing her to everyone she met. Elizabeth watched with pride as her friend easily mingled with the assembled company, her laughter ringing out like a melody.

James, who had been deep in conversation with Darcy, found his gaze frequently drifting towards Helen. He was captivated by her beauty and intelligence, and there was something about her that intrigued him deeply. After a while, he excused himself and made his way over to where Helen stood, engaged in a lively discussion with a group of guests.

"Miss Baxter," James greeted her with a smile. "I hope you are enjoying your evening."

Helen turned to him, her eyes sparkling with delight. "I am indeed, Sir. Pemberley is a most enchanting place, and the company is equally delightful."

"I am glad to hear that," James replied, his eyes never leaving hers. "May I have the honour of a dance?"

Helen's smile widened. "I would be delighted, Sir."

As they moved to the centre of the room, the musicians struck up a lively tune, and the guests formed a circle around the dancing couple. Elizabeth watched with keen interest as James and Helen began to dance, their movements perfectly in line with each other.

There was an undeniable chemistry between them, a connection that seemed to grow stronger with each step.

Darcy joined Elizabeth, observing the couple with a thoughtful expression. "It seems our guests have taken quite a liking to each other," he remarked.

"Indeed," Elizabeth agreed, a smile playing on her lips. "I have not seen Helen this animated in a long time. James appears to have made quite an impression."

As the dance continued, Helen and James spoke in hushed tones, their laughter mingling with the music. They moved with an effortless grace, their eyes never straying far from each other. By the time the dance ended, it was clear to everyone present that something special was blossoming between them.

Later in the evening, as the guests began to disperse, James found a quiet moment with Helen on the terrace. The night was cool, and the stars shone brightly overhead, casting a magical glow on the gardens below.

"I must confess, Miss Baxter" James began, his voice soft and earnest, "I have been captivated by you from the moment we met. Over the last couple of days, there is something about you that draws me in, something I cannot quite explain."

Helen felt her heart race at his words. "And I must admit, Sir, that I have felt a similar pull towards you. It is as if we were meant to meet."

James took her hand in his, his touch sending a thrill through her. "I believe that sometimes, fate has a way of bringing people together. And I cannot help but feel that you and I are destined for something extraordinary."

Helen gazed into his eyes, her own filled with a mixture of hope and excitement. "I feel the same."

As they stood there, hand in hand under the starlit sky, Elizabeth watched from a distance, her heart swelling with happiness for her friend. It seemed that Helen had found something special at Pemberley, and Elizabeth couldn't have been more pleased.

___The Return of Lydia

The days that followed were filled with joyous moments and budding romance. Helen and James spent much of their time together, exploring the beautiful grounds of Pemberley, engaging in spirited conversations, and sharing countless laughs. Their connection deepened with each passing day, and it was clear to all who observed them that they were falling in love.

Elizabeth watched their relationship blossom with great satisfaction. She had hoped that Helen would find someone who appreciated her for who she was, and James seemed to be that person. His genuine affection and admiration for Helen were evident in every glance and word.

One afternoon, as Elizabeth, Georgiana and Helen were walking through the rose garden, a letter arrived for Elizabeth. She opened it with a mix of curiosity and apprehension, recognising the handwriting immediately. It was from her younger sister, Lydia.

"Lydia writes that she wishes to visit Pemberley," Elizabeth informed Helen, her tone cautious. "She and her husband, Mr. Wickham, are planning to travel in this direction and hope to stay with us for a few days."

Helen raised an eyebrow. She had heard enough about Lydia and Mr. Wickham to know that their visits were often accompanied by drama and turmoil, in the letters exchanged between them. "Do you think it wise to have them here, given the current circumstances?" she asked gently.

Elizabeth sighed. "Lydia is my sister, and despite her many flaws, she is family. Fitzwilliam and I have tried to support her as best we can, though it has not always been easy. We shall have to manage as best we can. looking at Georgiana, "Don't worry Georgiana, I'm sure all will be well".

When Darcy learned of Lydia's impending visit, he was less than pleased, but he agreed that family obligations must be honoured. They prepared for Lydia's arrival, hoping that her stay would be uneventful, his guard for his sister, Georgiana, immediately arose whenever, the name of Wickham, was mentioned.

A few days later, Lydia and Mr. Wickham arrived at Pemberley. Lydia was as vivacious and impetuous as ever, her energy seeming to fill every room she entered. Mr. Wickham, on the other hand, carried an air of disinterest and thinly veiled resentment, clearly uncomfortable in the grand surroundings of Pemberley.

"Lizzy!" Lydia exclaimed, rushing to embrace her sister. "It is so wonderful to see you! And Pemberley is even more magnificent than I remembered."

"It is good to see you too, Lydia," Elizabeth replied, though her tone was more reserved. "I trust your journey was pleasant?"

"Oh, it was simply dreadful," Lydia declared, waving a hand dismissively. "But now that we are here, I intend to make the most of it."

As the introductions were made, Helen observed the interactions with keen interest. It was evident that Lydia was a force of nature, her presence impossible to ignore. Mr.

Wickham, meanwhile, seemed to sulk in the background, his expression one of perpetual dissatisfaction.

Despite the initial awkwardness, the household settled into a routine. Lydia's exuberance provided a stark contrast to the more refined atmosphere of Pemberley, but everyone did their best to accommodate her.

One evening, as the group gathered in the drawing room, Lydia's curiosity got the better of her. She had noticed the frequent and seemingly significant glances exchanged between Helen and James, and she could not resist probing into the matter.

"Helen, do tell," Lydia began with a mischievous smile. "What is going on between you and Lord Percy? You seem to be spending an awful lot of time together."

Helen blushed, caught off guard by Lydia's directness. "We have become good friends, Lydia," she replied, trying to keep her tone light. "He is a very kind and interesting gentleman."

Lydia's eyes sparkled with intrigue. "Oh, I see. Just friends, is it? Well, I think there is more to it than that. Don't you agree, Lord Percy?"

James, who had been listening quietly, smiled at Helen. "I do indeed value Miss Baxter's friendship very much," he said, his voice steady. "And I believe we have found a deep connection that goes beyond mere friendship."

Lydia clapped her hands in delight. "How exciting! I knew there was something more between you two. Well, I shall have to keep an eye on this developing romance."

Elizabeth, sensing that Lydia's meddling could lead to complications, decided to intervene. "Lydia, let us not pry into matters that are not our concern," she said firmly. "Helen and James deserve their privacy."

Lydia pouted but relented, her curiosity momentarily satisfied. The evening continued without further incident, but

Elizabeth couldn't shake the feeling that Lydia's presence might stir up trouble.

Turbulent Times

As the days went by, Lydia's disruptive influence became more apparent. She had a knack for creating tension and drama, often at the most inopportune moments. Her reckless behaviour and careless remarks put everyone on edge, and Elizabeth found herself constantly trying to smooth over the conflicts that arose.

Helen and James, however, remained largely unaffected by the turmoil. They continued to spend time together, their bond growing stronger with each passing day. James admired Helen's grace and resilience, and Helen found comfort and joy in James's steady presence.

One afternoon, as Helen and James were walking by the lake, they were joined by Mr. Wickham, who had been wandering the grounds aimlessly. He seemed to take a sudden interest in their conversation, his manner unusually cordial.

"Good day, Miss Baxter, Lord Percy," Wickham greeted them with a smile that did not reach his eyes. "I hope you are enjoying this fine weather."

"We are, Mr. Wickham," James replied politely, though he was wary of Wickham's intentions. "Is there something we can help you with?"

Wickham chuckled. "Oh, nothing in particular. I was just admiring the beauty of Pemberley and thought I might join you for a while. It is always pleasant to have company, don't you agree?"

Helen sensed the underlying tension in Wickham's tone and decided to steer the conversation in a different direction.

"Pemberley is indeed a beautiful place," she said. "I have enjoyed exploring its many wonders."

Wickham nodded, his gaze shifting between Helen and James. "It must be lovely to spend time with such agreeable company.

Miss Baxter, you seem to have found a true friend in Lord Percy".

"I am fortunate to have many good friends," Helen replied, her voice steady. "James has been a wonderful companion."

As they continued their walk, Wickham's attempts to insinuate himself into their conversation became more transparent. He made several veiled comments about the nature of their relationship, his tone growing increasingly insinuative.

James, who had been patient up until this point, finally decided to address Wickham directly. "Mr. Wickham, if you have something to say, I suggest you do so plainly," he said, his voice firm. "I do not appreciate insinuations or attempts to cause discord."

Wickham feigned surprise. "Oh, I meant no harm, my Lord, I was merely making conversation. It seems I have overstepped my bounds."

"Indeed," James replied curtly. "Now, if you will excuse us, Miss Baxter and I have matters to discuss."

Wickham took the hint and departed, leaving Helen and James alone once more. Helen let out a sigh of relief. "Thank you, James. I was beginning to feel quite uncomfortable."

"I am sorry you had to endure that," James said, his expression softening. "Wickham has a way of causing trouble wherever he goes. But I will not allow him to disturb our time together."

Helen smiled, grateful for James's support. "I appreciate that more than you know. Let us put this unpleasant encounter behind us and enjoy the rest of our day."

As they continued their walk, the bond between them grew even stronger, fortified by the challenges they faced together.

Revelations and Resolutions

The visit of Lydia and Mr. Wickham continued to test the patience of everyone at Pemberley. Elizabeth found herself constantly mediating disputes and soothing ruffled feathers, while Darcy did his best to remain civil despite his deep- seated dislike for Wickham.

One evening, as the household gathered for dinner, Lydia's behaviour took a particularly troubling turn. She had indulged in more wine than was prudent and began to speak more freely than usual. Her remarks grew increasingly bold and inappropriate, causing discomfort among the guests.

"Lydia, perhaps you should retire for the evening," Elizabeth suggested gently, hoping to avoid further embarrassment.

"Nonsense, Lizzy," Lydia replied with a dismissive wave of her hand. "I am perfectly fine. In fact, I have something important to say."

Elizabeth's heart sank, knowing that nothing good could come from Lydia's current state. "Lydia, please..."

But Lydia was undeterred. She turned her attention to Helen and James, a sly smile playing on her lips. "Miss Baxter, Lord Percy, you seem quite taken with each other. Tell me, is there something more between you than mere friendship?"

Helen felt her cheeks flush with embarrassment, and James's expression hardened. "Lydia, this is neither the time nor the place for such questions," he said sternly.

But Lydia was not to be dissuaded. "Oh, come now, James. We are all friends here. Surely there is no harm in a little curiosity. After all, we are all wondering what the future holds for you two."

Elizabeth could see the strain in Helen's eyes and the anger in James's. She decided to intervene. "Lydia, that is enough. You are being very rude, and I must insist that you apologise."

Lydia pouted, clearly displeased with being reprimanded. "Oh, very well. I am sorry if I have offended anyone." But her tone lacked sincerity, and the damage was done.

The rest of the evening passed in awkward silence, and Elizabeth knew that something had to be done. The next morning, she spoke with Darcy, and they decided that it was time for Lydia and Mr. Wickham to leave Pemberley.

When Elizabeth informed Lydia of their decision, her sister was indignant. "You cannot be serious, Lizzy! We are family, and you are throwing us out?"

"Lydia, this visit has caused nothing but trouble," Elizabeth replied firmly. "You and Mr. Wickham must leave. We will provide for your travel arrangements and ensure you have a place to stay, but you cannot remain here."

"At least, let's all have a ride together, your grounds are so lovely and we all like riding and it will help to depart, on more pleasant terms" Lydia's eyes wide open, looking at her sister.

"Lydia! Please, let me think about it". Elizabeth said. Lydia stormed off in a huff.

No, Elizabeth's mind was set about them leaving. But maybe to calm thesituation, a ride might help. She would talk with Fitzwilliam later.

It was arranged for Lydia and Mr Wickham, to leave Pemberley the next day. Elizabeth had spoken with Fitzwilliam, his sister, together with Lord Percy and Helen and agreed to go for a ride late morning before luncheon, before their departure in the afternoon. Elizabeth suggested it hoping the fresh air and splendid scenery would provide some relief, for all.

Mr. Darcy, ever attentive to his wife's needs and recognising the necessity of restoring harmony, agreed readily. However, Georgiana Darcy, still uneasy around the tumultuous Lydia and Wickham, chose to remain home. The party thus consisted of Mr. Darcy, Elizabeth, Lord Percy and Miss Helen Baxter, Lydia, and Mr. Wickham.

As they set out in the fresh morning air, the initial tension began to dissipate, giving way to the rhythm of hooves and the beauty of the surrounding nature. Riding alongside her husband, Elizabeth felt a semblance of peace return.

The vast fields and meticulously maintained trails of Pemberley provided a serene backdrop, temporarily distracting everyone from the underlying discord. However, it wasn't long before Mr. Wickham's propensity for trouble resurfaced.

As the group approached a series of jumps, Wickham, eager to show off and perhaps to needle Mr. Darcy, spurred his horse forward recklessly. Lord Percy, an accomplished horseman, followed suit, though with more grace and control. The rest of the group watched with a mixture of concern and amusement.

"What a show-off," muttered Lord Percy, his disdain for Wickham barely concealed.

Wickham, overhearing, shot back, "Jealousy, Percy? Surely not becoming of a gentleman."

The exchange quickly escalated into a heated argument, their voices rising above the thudding hooves. In the midst of this, Wickham's horse approached a high jump. Distracted by the quarrel, Wickham failed to steady his mount properly. The horse balked at the obstacle, rearing up and throwing Wickham off with a violent jolt.

The scene unfolded in slow motion for Elizabeth. Wickham landed awkwardly, his head striking a rock. The reins became entangled around his limbs as the startled horse bolted, dragging him along. Shouts of alarm echoed through the air as the group rushed to his aid.

Mr. Darcy and Lord Percy were the first to reach Wickham, but it was too late. The sight was gruesome, Wickham's lifeless body lay crumpled, blood seeping from a head wound. His eyes were closed, face pallid, a stark contrast to the vibrant life that had so recently sparked with indignation.

Lydia, upon seeing her husband's lifeless form, let out a piercing scream. She fell to her knees, shaking uncontrollably. Elizabeth dismounted swiftly, rushing to her sister's side, trying to offer what little comfort she could.

"What are we to do?" Lydia wailed, her voice a mixture of grief and panic. "He can't be dead! He can't!"

Mr. Darcy, though troubled by Wickham's past transgressions, maintained his composure. "We must return to the house and send for a doctor," he said gravely. "Though I fear it is too late."

Helen Baxter, pale but resolute, took Lydia's arm. "Come, Lydia. Let us return to the house," she urged gently. Lydia, stunned and disoriented, allowed herself to be led away.

As the group made their somber way back to Pemberley, Elizabeth couldn't help but reflect on the tragic turn of events. Wickham's death, though it removed a source of strife, brought with it new complications and sorrows, especially for Lydia. The following days would be difficult, but with Mr.Darcy by her side, Elizabeth felt a glimmer of hope that they would navigate this new crisis together.

Once back at the house, Mr. Darcy quickly dispatched a message for the doctor and the funeral director. The solemn task fell heavily upon him, but his usual resolve did not falter. Elizabeth, her heart aching for her sister, took it upon herself to inform Georgiana of the tragic events.

The young girl, though distressed, bore the news with a quiet strength, her bond with Elizabeth providing some comfort.

Helen Baxter remained with a distraught Lydia, her presence a calming influence amid the chaos. Lydia's sobs echoed through the corridors of Pemberley, a stark reminder of the fragility of life. Elizabeth composed herself as best she could and sent urgent messages to her parents and sister Jane, conveying the dreadful event with as much care as the written word allowed.

As the day waned into evening, both James and Helen Baxter approached Elizabeth and Darcy with heavy hearts. "I shall leave in the morning," James announced softly. Elizabeth felt a pang of disappointment, the departure of them both, a loss in this time of turmoil, but she understood their need to return to their own lives.

"I am sorry to see you go," Elizabeth replied, her voice steady. "But I understand. Thank you for all your support."

Helen squeezed Elizabeth's hand. "I am sure we both wish you strength in the coming days."

Elizabeth managed a grateful smile, her mind already turning to the myriad responsibilities awaiting her. She spoke with Mrs. Reynolds, Pemberley's housekeeper, about putting the estate into mourning. Mrs. Reynolds, ever efficient and compassionate, reassured Elizabeth, "Do not worry, Mrs.Darcy. I will see to everything."

Lydia, isolated in her grief, eventually turned to Elizabeth with a heart-wrenching question. "What will happen to me now?" she asked, her voice trembling.

Elizabeth hugged her sister, offering what little comfort she could. "My dear dear sister, we shall take care of everything. We will find out what Mr. Wickham has left you," she said, though she feared the worst.

Darcy went through Wickham's papers, once received. His face grew grimmer with each passing minute. When he finally rejoined Elizabeth, the news was as dire as she had feared.

"

Lydia is penniless," Darcy said quietly. "Wickham left nothing behind but debts."

Elizabeth's heart sank. She knew Lydia's predicament would weigh heavily on her family. "We will have to take care of her," she said resolutely. "She cannot be left destitute."

Darcy nodded, his admiration for his wife's unwavering compassion clear in his eyes. "We will do what we must," he agreed. "Pemberley will be her home as long as she needs it."

The days that followed were filled with sorrow and duty. The doctor confirmed what they already knew: Mr. Wickham had died instantly from his injuries. The funeral was arranged, and would be a muted affair, attended by close family and a few friends, the weight of Wickham's past indiscretions casting a long shadow.

The following day, Mr. and Mrs. Bennet arrived at Pemberley to console Lydia. Mrs. Bennet, her usual exuberance tempered by the somber occasion, fussed over her youngest daughter, while Mr. Bennet remained more subdued, observing quietly.

"Lydia, my dear, such a terrible misfortune!" Mrs. Bennet exclaimed, dabbing her eyes with a handkerchief. "I always suspected Mr. Wickham was a rogue, but who could resist such a handsome man in his regimentals?"

Mr. Bennet, standing slightly apart, watched his wife's familiar theatrics with a resigned expression. His concern for Lydia was evident, though he expressed it through quiet support rather than words.

Shortly after, Jane and Mr. Bingley arrived, Jane's radiant presence bringing a touch of joy to the otherwise gloomy atmosphere. Her pregnancy added a glow to her cheeks, and Elizabeth felt a surge of happiness at seeing her sister so content.

"Oh, Jane, how wonderful to see you," Elizabeth said, embracing her sister. "Congratulations, Charles, I was overwhelmed by the new, we are so happy for you both" Elizabeth said embracing her brother in law.

"Thank you, I am sure you shall be making an announcement soon yourselves!" Charles said with a smile.

"Thank you, Lizzy," Jane replied warmly. "I only wish we were here under better circumstances."

Their reunion was bittersweet, the joy of seeing family mingled with the sadness of recent events. Mrs. Bennet, never one to miss an opportunity for conversation, was soon engrossed in a lively discussion with her sister, Mrs. Philips, who also attended, about Wickham's dashing appearance and lamentable character.

Mrs. Bennet, in a fit of agitation, relayed to her sister, Mrs. Phillips, the troubling news her maid had recently divulged about Mr. Wickham's time at Pemberley. According to the maid, Mr. Wickham had shown himself to be a man of considerable moral failings, engaging in behaviour that left no gentlemen's daughter safe from his unscrupulous advances.

His conduct was further marred by financial irresponsibility, as he accumulated debts with reckless abandon, tarnishing his reputation and casting a shadow over the household.

Mrs. Bennet's account, coloured with a mixture of indignation and vindication, highlighted her concern for the young women who had the misfortune of crossing paths with such a disreputable character, particularly her poor Lydia. Mrs Phillips agreed with her.

"He was always so charming, but I knew there was something not quite right about him, but no one listened to me," Mrs. Bennet declared, shaking her head. "Such a pity."

The next morning it was clear and bright, when Helen and James prepared to leave Pemberley. After a quiet breakfast, a groom brought Lord Percy's horse around to the front of the house. Just behind, a carriage that Mr. Darcy had arranged waited to take Helen back to her Norfolk home.

Elizabeth, with her husband and Georgiana, walked with them towards the entrance door. The sun shone warmly, and the air was crisp and dry. The group paused to express their thanks and best wishes towards Lydia.

"Thank you both for coming," Elizabeth said sincerely. "Your presence has meant a great deal to all of us."

Darcy added, "We insist you both return to Pemberley one day. You are always welcome here."

Helen smiled, her gaze turning to Georgiana. "I look forward to playing the pianoforte with you again, Georgiana. Perhaps next time we can play a duet?"

Georgiana returned the smile warmly. "I would love that, Helen. Safe travels."

Lord Percy and Helen descended the steps of Pemberley. As they reached the bottom, Lord Percy took Helen's hand. "It has been a pleasure meeting you, Helen," he said earnestly. "I must return to the north, but may I write to you?"

Helen's cheeks flushed slightly, and she nodded. "I would be delighted to hear from you, Lord Percy."

With a gentle kiss to her hand, Lord Percy helped Helen into her carriage. He then mounted his horse, his eyes lingering on her for a moment longer.

Everyone waved goodbye as the carriage and horse set off in their different directions. Elizabeth stood beside Darcy, watching the carriage until it disappeared down the lane. She couldn't help but wonder what the two had said to each other and hoped that it wasn't the end of their acquaintance.

Later, in her carriage, Helen's mind was filled with thoughts of all that had transpired at Pemberley. The sadness of recent events mingled with the joy of new friendships and budding affection. She eagerly anticipated sharing everything with her parents once she arrived home. Her thoughts kept returning to Lord Percy, and she wondered if their paths would cross again.

Elizabeth, standing beside Darcy, took his hand. "Do you think we'll see them again?" she asked, her eyes following the path the carriage had taken.

"I have no doubt," Darcy replied. "True connections are never easily severed."

Elizabeth smiled, feeling the truth of his words. With Darcy by her side and the love of her family, she felt ready to face whatever the future held.

As for Lord Percy, he rode across the fields with a sense of exhilaration. His thoughts drifted away from the recent sorrows, focusing instead on the captivating creature that Helen was and how she had captured his heart. The anticipation of writing to her and possibly seeing her again filled him with excitement.

Later that day, back at Pemberley, Mr. and Mrs. Gardiner arrived, their presence a welcome addition. Mr. Darcy remembered them fondly from their earlier visit to Pemberley, before his marriage to Elizabeth, and greeted them warmly.

"Mr. Gardiner, Mrs. Gardiner, it is good to see you again, despite the circumstances," Darcy said, shaking Mr. Gardiner's hand.

"Thank you, Mr. Darcy," Mrs. Gardiner replied. "We are here to support Lydia and the family as best we can." Darcy enjoyed seeing them again.

Darcy and Elizabeth took the opportunity to discuss Lydia's future with her parents. They explained that Lydia was penniless and would need support until her future could be decided.

"

She can stay with us at Pemberley for as long as she needs," Darcy offered, his tone firm but kind.

Mrs. Bennet, her maternal instincts kicking in, protested immediately. "Lydia must come back with us to Longbourn after the funeral. It is her home, and she will need her family close by."

Mr. Bennet, who had been silent until now, nodded in agreement. "Your mother is right. Lydia should be with us, where we can keep an eye on her."

Elizabeth, understanding her parents' concern but also knowing the challenges they faced, tried to mediate. "Perhaps, after some time at Pemberley, we can reassess the situation.

Lydia will need to heal, and Pemberley offers a quiet place for her to do that."

Mrs. Gardiner, ever practical, added, "Let us take it one step at a time. Lydia's well-being is the most important thing right now."

The Bennett's reluctantly agreed to this arrangement, recognising the wisdom in giving Lydia some space to recover from her ordeal. The funeral, a somber affair, brought a sense of finality. The Bennet family, along with the Darcys and their friends, stood united in their grief and support for Lydia.

In the days that followed, the presence of her family and the tranquil environment of Pemberley began to have a positive effect on Lydia. She found solace in the company of her sisters and the steady support of Mr. Darcy. Though the future remained uncertain, there was a renewed sense of hope.

Elizabeth, ever perceptive, noticed the subtle changes in her sister's manner. "Lydia, you are stronger than you realise," she said one evening as they walked through the gardens.

Lydia, still fragile but beginning to heal, managed a small smile. "With all of you here, I feel I can face whatever comes next."

The family's unity and love provided a foundation upon which Lydia could rebuild her life. And in the heart of Pemberley, amidst the trials and tribulations, there was a promise of new beginnings and the enduring strength of family bonds.

The gathering stayed at Pemberley for a few more days, providing Lydia with much-needed support and solace. The serene environment and the presence of her family helped her begin to heal. Eventually, Lydia returned to Longbourn with her parents, while Jane, Mr. Bingley, and the Gardiner's also departed for their respective homes.

Longbourn

A few weeks later, Elizabeth decided to visit Longbourn to see how her sister and parents were faring. She found the house quieter than usual, a subtle melancholy lingering in the air.

Mrs. Bennet was more subdued, her usual flurry of complaints and worries tempered by the recent tragedy. Mr. Bennet, though still reserved, seemed more attentive to Lydia, who was slowly adjusting to her new reality.

Elizabeth and Lydia decided to take a walk around the garden, enjoying the crisp air and the vibrant colours of late spring.

Their conversation started light, discussing the blooming flowers and the latest news from Meryton. However, Elizabeth noticed a contemplative look on Lydia's face, a depth of thought that was uncharacteristic of her usually carefree sister.

After a pause, Lydia turned to Elizabeth and said, "I have been a fool, haven't I, Lizzy? I should have never run off with him."

Elizabeth, though surprised by the admission, felt a surge of empathy for her sister. "You were young, Lydia. He took advantage of your naivety. But yes, running off with him was a mistake."

Lydia sighed, a mix of regret and resignation in her expression. "It's over now, I suppose. I have to move on."

Elizabeth took Lydia's hand, squeezing it gently. "Yes, it's over. What matters now is how you choose to move forward.

You have your family here to support you, and you are stronger than you think."

Lydia nodded, her eyes reflecting a newfound determination. "Thank you, Lizzy."

That night, back at Pemberley, Elizabeth shared the conversation with Darcy. They were sitting by the fireplace, the warmth and comfort of the room contrasting with the heavy topics they discussed.

"Lydia said something surprising today," Elizabeth began, recounting her sister's unexpected remark.

Darcy listened intently, his brow furrowing in thought. "Perhaps this ordeal has given her a chance to reflect and mature," he suggested.

"I hope so," Elizabeth replied. "She seems to understand now that she made a mistake. I just want her to find peace and stability."

Darcy nodded, taking Elizabeth's hand in his. "With time, she will. The issues with Wickham are finally over, and we can all begin to move forward."

Elizabeth leaned into her husband's embrace, feeling the solid strength of his presence. "Thank you for everything, Fitzwilliam. Your support means the world to me and my family."

Darcy kissed her forehead, his love and reassurance palpable. "We are a family, Elizabeth. We face these challenges together."

As they sat together, the fire crackling softly, Elizabeth felt a profound sense of gratitude. Despite the recent sorrows, she knew that with Darcy by her side, they could overcome any adversity. Lydia's acknowledgment of her past mistakes was a hopeful sign of her growth, and Elizabeth believed that, surrounded by her loving family, her sister would find her way to a better future.

Pemberley stood as a symbol of resilience and renewal, a place where love and family could heal even the deepest wounds.

And in that moment, Elizabeth embraced not only her husband but also the promise of brighter days ahead.

Mrs. Darcy's Christmas

The first snow of the season had begun to fall, blanketing the vast grounds of Pemberley in a shimmering layer of white.

Inside the grand estate, Elizabeth Darcy stood by the window, her fingers gently tracing the frosty patterns on the glass.

The year had been one of unexpected events, and as she watched the snowflakes dance in the winter breeze, she felt a mix of anticipation and apprehension about the upcoming Christmas.

Elizabeth turned from the window and made her way to the drawing room, where her husband, Fitzwilliam Darcy, was engrossed in a book. She admired the peaceful expression on his face, one that had been absent for some time.

The tragic death of Mr. Wickham had cast a shadow over Pemberley, and they had spent the past few months in quiet reflection. But now, with Christmas approaching, Elizabeth felt it was time to bring joy and laughter back to their home.

Fitzwilliam," she said softly, taking a seat beside him, "I have been thinking."

Darcy looked up from his book, his eyes meeting hers with a warm, curious gaze. "And what has occupied your thoughts, my dear?"

"I believe it is time we gathered our family and friends here at Pemberley for Christmas," Elizabeth suggested, her voice filled with a hopeful lilt. "It would be good to have everyone together."

Darcy considered her words, his expression thoughtful. The last time they had hosted such a gathering was under grim circumstances.

However, the idea of filling Pemberley with the people they loved, the sound of laughter echoing through the halls, was a tempting one.

"

"You are right, Elizabeth," he agreed with a nod. "It would be wonderful to have everyone here. Georgiana would be delighted as well."

Elizabeth smiled, her heart lightening at his approval. Georgiana, Darcy's younger sister, had indeed agreed with her, that a grand Christmas gathering would lift everyone's spirits. The decision was made, and soon invitations were sent out to their nearest and dearest.

Among the first to be invited were the Bennett's. Elizabeth was eager to see her parents and sisters again, especially Jane, who had recently given birth to a beautiful daughter named

Charlotte Jane Bingley. Elizabeth had only seen her niece once, and she was now three months old and utterly adorable.

The Bingley's including Mr. Bingley's sisters, were also invited. Elizabeth hoped that their presence would bring joy to Pemberley, as they always did with their lively company. The Gardiner's Elizabeth's beloved aunt and uncle, and their children were next on the list. Elizabeth had fond memories of their tour of the Lakes, and she looked forward to seeing how much their children had grown.

Lady Catherine de Bourgh, Darcy's formidable aunt, was extended an invitation, though Elizabeth was not surprised when she declined, citing prior engagements. Colonel Fitzwilliam, whom Elizabeth had only seen once since their walk at Rosings Park, was invited and graciously accepted.

Mrs. Phillips, Mr. and Mrs. Collins, Helen Baxter and her parents, and Lord Percy were also on the guest list. Elizabeth was particularly eager to see Helen, as she had received letters from her over the past months, and it seemed her relationship with Lord Percy was blossoming nicely. She was pleased that Lord Percy had accepted their invitation and hoped to learn more about their budding romance.

Elizabeth's thoughts also turned to her younger sisters, Mary and Kitty. She knew that Kitty had recently secured a position as a governess and was eager to hear about her experiences.

Elizabeth was also curious about Lydia, whose life had been tumultuous after Wickham's death. According to her mother, Mrs. Bennet, Lydia had begun to change for the better, forming a friendship with the son of the clergyman in the next parish to Longbourn. Elizabeth hoped to see this transformation for herself.

As the invitations were sent out and preparations began in earnest, the halls of Pemberley slowly filled with the spirit of Christmas. Evergreen garlands adorned the bannisters, and the scent of pine mingled with the aroma of baking pastries wafted from the kitchens. The grand tree in the drawing room sparkled with candles and ornaments, a testament to the care and effort that Elizabeth and Georgiana had put into making this Christmas a special one.

When the guests began to arrive, Pemberley came alive with the sounds of reunion and merriment. The Bennet's were among the first to arrive, bringing with them an air of familiarity and warmth. Elizabeth was glad to see her parents again.

Next to arrive were Charles and Jane, with baby Charlotte in her arms. Jane looked radiant, and Elizabeth felt a surge of affection for her elder sister, their entrance marked by the cheerful chatter of Mr. Bingley and the polite, though somewhat stiff, greetings from his sisters.

"Elizabeth!" Jane exclaimed, embracing her tightly.

"I am happy to see you," Elizabeth replied, her eyes shining with happiness. "And how is little Charlotte. She is absolutely precious."

The Gardiner's arrived shortly after, their children rushing forward to greet Elizabeth with excited smiles.

Colonel Fitzwilliam's arrival brought a sense of camaraderie, his easy manners and good humour quickly putting everyone at ease. He and Darcy fell into a comfortable conversation, reminiscing about their shared experiences and catching up on the latest news.

Helen Baxter and her parents, along with Lord Percy, were warmly welcomed has their carriage pulled up and came to a halt.

Elizabeth noticed the subtle glances and smiles exchanged between Helen and Lord Percy, and she hoped that their relationship had continued to flourish.

Mary and Kitty arrived together with Lydia, bringing with them news of their lives. Kitty spoke animatedly about her position as a governess, while Mary shared her latest musical compositions. Lydia was more subdued, but Elizabeth could see a change in her sister's manner. She seemed more thoughtful and composed, and her friendship with the clergyman's son had clearly had a positive influence on her.

The days leading up to Christmas were filled with activities and preparations. There were morning walks through the snow covered grounds, afternoons spent decorating and baking, and evenings filled with music and conversation by the fire.

Elizabeth found herself caught up in the joy of the season, her heart swelling with gratitude for the family and friends gathered at Pemberley.

On Christmas Eve, a grand feast was held in the dining room, the table laden with a sumptuous array of dishes. There was laughter and lively conversation as everyone gathered around, sharing stories and memories. Darcy, seated at the head of the table, looked around at the assembled guests, his heart full.

"Elizabeth," he said quietly, reaching for her hand, "this was a wonderful idea. Thank you."

Elizabeth smiled, squeezing his hand gently. "It is all the more special because we are surrounded by those we love."

The evening continued with music and dancing in the drawing room. Georgiana played the piano beautifully, her music filling the room with a sense of serenity and joy. Colonel Fitzwilliam joined her in a duet, their performance met with enthusiastic applause.

As the clock struck midnight, the guests gathered around the grand tree to exchange gifts. There were exclamations of delight and heartfelt thanks as presents were opened, the room filled with the warmth of shared happiness.

Christmas Day dawned bright and clear, the sun shining on the snow covered landscape. The guests attended a service at the local church, where the choir's voices rang out in joyful harmony. The sense of community and togetherness was palpable, and Elizabeth felt a deep sense of contentment.

Back at Pemberley, the festivities continued with a traditional Christmas dinner, followed by a Servants' Ball in the evening. Darcy and Elizabeth took the opportunity to express their gratitude to the staff, whose hard work and dedication had made the holiday season so special. The ball was a joyous affair, with music, dancing, and laughter filling the air.

The highlight of the celebrations was the grand Christmas Ball, held for family, friends, and members of high society with connections to Pemberley. The guests arrived in their finest attire, the ballroom sparkling with candlelight and

festive decorations. Elizabeth, resplendent in a gown of deep green velvet, moved through the room with grace and elegance, her smile radiant.

As the evening progressed, Elizabeth couldn't help but notice the growing affection between Helen and Lord Percy. They danced together several times, their connection evident in the way they looked at each other. Elizabeth felt a sense of satisfaction, knowing that love was blossoming at Pemberley.

Georgiana, too, was in high spirits, enjoying the company of Colonel Fitzwilliam. The two shared several dances, their camaraderie bringing a smile to Elizabeth's face. She was pleased to see her sister so happy and at ease.

Mr. and Mrs. Baxter took the opportunity to learn more about the Percy and Darcy families. They discovered that Lord Percy, though the youngest son, had a distinguished brother, Edward, married to Victoria, who would inherit the title and estate. Lord Percy's sister, Louisa, was intended to marry Lord Bellingham, adding another layer of connection between the families.

The evening was a resounding success, the joy and laughter lasting long into the night. As the guests began to depart, Elizabeth felt a deep sense of fulfilment. The Christmas celebrations had brought everyone together, strengthening bonds and creating new memories.

As the year drew to a close, Elizabeth reflected on the journey they had taken. The past months had been marked by sorrow and reflection, but also by growth and renewal. Pemberley had once again become a place of joy and love, its halls filled with the laughter and warmth of family and friends.

The Coming of The New Year

On New Year's Eve, Elizabeth gathered the guests in the drawing room for a special announcement. The room fell silent as she stood beside Darcy, her eyes shining with excitement.

"My dear friends," she began, her voice steady and clear, "I have wonderful news to share. Fitzwilliam and I are expecting a child." A chorus of delighted exclamations filled the room as the news sank in. Darcy's expression was one of pride and joy, his hand resting protectively on Elizabeth's shoulder.

"This is the best possible way to start the new year," Jane said, embracing her sister."Congratulations, Elizabeth. We are all so happy for you."

"Indeed," Mr. Bennet agreed, his eyes twinkling with affection. "A new addition to the Darcy family is truly a cause for celebration. Another grandchild we will have Mrs Bennet." He proclaimed.

The news added an extra layer of joy to the already festive atmosphere. Toasts were raised, and the room buzzed with excitement and well wishes. Elizabeth felt overwhelmed with happiness, her heart full of gratitude for the love and support of those around her.

As midnight approached, the guests gathered in the great hall to ring in the new year. The clock struck twelve, and a chorus of voices joined together to sing "Auld Lang Syne," the familiar tune resonating through the halls of Pemberley. The new year was welcomed with cheers and embraces, the new year of 1815 began with the promise of fresh beginnings and continued joy.

After the guests had all departed, the echoes of their laughter and the warmth of their presence lingered in the halls of Pemberley. Life settled into a peaceful routine, with the rhythms of the estate aligning with the needs of the expected newest member of the Darcy family.

Elizabeth stood with Darcy by her side, their hands entwined as they looked out at their family and friends. The past year had been one of trials and tribulations, but it had also brought them closer together.

They had faced challenges, and they had found strength in each other.

The months that followed were filled with anticipation and preparation. Pemberley buzzed with activity as plans were made for the arrival of the new baby. Elizabeth's friends and family were a constant source of support, their visits bringing joy and comfort.

Helen Baxter and Lord Percy continued to grow closer, their relationship blossoming into a deep and abiding love.

Elizabeth was delighted when they announced their engagement, knowing that Pemberley had played a role in bringing them together.

Georgiana's friendship with Colonel Fitzwilliam also deepened. The colonel's visits became more frequent, and it was clear to all that a special bond was forming between them. Elizabeth watched with a mixture of pride and hope, knowing that Georgiana had found someone who truly appreciated her gentle spirit and kind heart.

Summer arrived, bringing with it a sense of renewal and new beginnings. The gardens of Pemberley bloomed in vibrant colours, a testament to the changing seasons. Elizabeth's pregnancy progressed smoothly, and she found joy in the preparations for the baby's arrival. The nursery was lovingly decorated, and tiny garments were carefully sewn and arranged.

One warm summer afternoon, as Elizabeth sat in the sunlit drawing room, she received a letter from Helen. The news was joyous: Helen and Lord Percy were to be married in the Autumn and they would be invited to Northumberland House, for the wedding. Elizabeth was overjoyed at the prospect, knowing that it would be a celebration of love and friendship.

As the day's passed, Elizabeth's anticipation grew. She cherished the moments spent with Darcy, their bond stronger than ever. They spoke often of their hopes and dreams for their growing family, their conversations filled with warmth and affection.

It was late summer, Pemberley was a hub of activity as preparations for the birth, time passed in a blur of happiness and anticipation. Elizabeth's pregnancy continued to progress smoothly, and she found herself surrounded by love and support. Jane visited often, who now was expecting another herself, bringing little

Charlotte, whose laughter filled the halls of Pemberley with joy.

One morning, Elizabeth felt the first pangs of labor. The household sprang into action, and Darcy remained by her side, his presence a source of strength and comfort.

After several hours, their child was born, a healthy baby boy with Darcy's dark eyes and Elizabeth's bright smile. They named him William Bennet Darcy, a tribute to the family that had shaped their lives.

As Elizabeth held her son for the first time, she felt an overwhelming sense of love and gratitude. This tiny new life was a symbol of hope and renewal, a testament to the journey they had taken together.

The news of William's birth spread quickly, and Pemberley was soon filled with visitors eager to meet the newest member of the Darcy family. Mr and Mrs Bennet were among the first to arrive, their faces alight with joy, as they peered curiously at the baby, wide eyes filled with wonder.

Mrs. Bennet, her usual fluttering manner tempered by genuine happiness, was overjoyed at the arrival of her grandson. "Oh, Elizabeth," she exclaimed, tears in her eyes, "he is perfect."

"Thank you, Mama," Elizabeth replied, her heart full.

As the weeks passed, Pemberley settled into a new rhythm, one that revolved around the needs of the newest Darcy.

Elizabeth found immense joy in caring for her son, and Darcy was a doting father, his love for William evident in every gesture.

Autumn arrived, with it changing colours, celebrations, weddings and birthdays. Elizabeth found time go by so quickly.

The holiday season, soon approached once more, Christmas at Pemberley was a time of celebration and gratitude. The estate was once again adorned with festive decorations, and the halls echoed with the sounds of laughter and music. Family and friends gathered to share in the joy of the season, their presence a testament to the enduring power of love and friendship.

On Christmas Eve, as they gathered around the grand tree, Elizabeth felt a deep sense of contentment. She looked around at the faces of those she loved, her heart swelling with gratitude.

Darcy stood beside her, holding William in his arms. He looked at Elizabeth, his eyes filled with love. "This has been the most wonderful year," he said softly. "I am so grateful for you, for our family, for everything."

Elizabeth smiled, her eyes misting with tears of happiness. "And I am grateful for you, Fitzwilliam. Our journey has been filled with unexpected twists, but it has brought us here, to this moment, surrounded by love."

As the clock struck midnight, signalling the arrival of Christmas Day, the guests raised their glasses in a toast. "To family," Mr. Bennet said, his voice resonant with emotion. "To love and to new beginnings."

The room echoed with cheers and heartfelt sentiments, the spirit of Christmas alive and well at Pemberley.

The celebrations continued long into the night, the joy and warmth of the season enveloping everyone in its embrace. Elizabeth and Darcy stood together, their hearts united in love and gratitude. They looked forward to the future, knowing that whatever challenges lay ahead, they would face them together, with their family and friends by their side.

And so, as the first light of Christmas morning filtered through the windows of Pemberley, Elizabeth held her son close, her heart full of hope and joy. This was their Christmas, a time of renewal and celebration, a testament to the enduring love.

Elizabeth found immense joy in the simple moments of motherhood: the soft coos of her baby, the way William's tiny fingers grasped hers, the gentle rise and fall of his chest as he slept. She often walked the halls of Pemberley with William in her arms, feeling a deep sense of connection to the history and future of the estate.

Darcy was a devoted father, his bond with William growing stronger each day. He cherished the quiet moments he spent with his son, reading to him from the vast library or simply holding him close. The sight of Darcy cradling their baby filled Elizabeth's heart with love and gratitude.

Spring arrived once again, bringing with it the promise of renewal. The gardens of Pemberley bloomed in vibrant colours, a testament to the enduring cycle of life. Elizabeth often found herself in the garden, her son nestled in her arms as she marvelled at the beauty of the flowers and the tranquility of the estate.

Darcy quickly approached Elizabeth, who was in the garden playing with their baby son, William. The late afternoon sun cast a warm glow on the scene, making the flowers around them appear even more vibrant.

With a gentle smile, Darcy caught her eye and said, "Elizabeth, I have wonderful news. A letter has just arrived, your sister Jane has given birth to a healthy baby boy!" Elizabeth's face lit up with joy as she picked up William, hugging him tightly while her eyes sparkled with happiness at the thought of her sister's newfound joy.

The End.

About the Author

Darryl Martel is a versatile author whose work spans various genres, including fiction, non-fiction, and poetry. With a keen eye for detail and a deep understanding of human emotions, Martel's writings often explore themes such as identity, resilience, and the intricacies of personal relationships. His storytelling is marked by rich, vivid descriptions and well-drawn characters that resonate with readers. Beyond his literary pursuits, Martel is also an avid traveler and cultural enthusiast, experiences that frequently influence and enrich his narrative style. His dedication to the craft of writing has earned him a dedicated following and critical acclaim in the literary community.

Information

Elizabeth Bennet and Fitzwilliam Darcy, beloved characters from Jane Austen's *Pride and Prejudice*, are icons of classic literature and have enchanted readers since the novel's publication in 1813. The story of their relationship has come to symbolize the triumph of love over pride and prejudice, embodying themes that resonate with readers across generations.

Jane Austen's England: The Regency Context

To understand Elizabeth and Darcy's story, it's essential to know the societal norms of Regency England, the era in which *Pride and Prejudice* is set. This period, spanning the early 19th century, was marked by strict class hierarchies, limited social mobility, and a deep emphasis on marriage as a social contract. Young women of the gentry class, like Elizabeth Bennet, were expected to marry well to secure their social and financial futures. Love was often secondary, if considered at all.

Against this backdrop, Elizabeth and Darcy's relationship unfolds with all the complexity of class, reputation, and social expectations. Jane Austen was acutely aware of these societal pressures, which she subtly critiques in her portrayal of Elizabeth and Darcy's struggle to find a common ground.

Elizabeth Bennet: Wit, Independence, and Strong Convictions

Elizabeth Bennet is one of literature's most enduring heroines. As the second eldest daughter of the Bennet family, she stands out for her wit, intelligence, and strong sense of self, despite her family's modest social standing. Unlike her mother, who is often portrayed as fixated on marrying off her daughters,

Elizabeth values personal compatibility and respect in marriage. Her refusal to marry Mr. Collins, a clergyman who proposes for convenience, demonstrates her desire for a genuine partnership rather than a relationship built solely on financial or social gain.

Elizabeth's charm and independence challenge the norms of her time. She is unafraid to speak her mind, even to people of higher social status. Her interactions with Mr. Darcy, in particular, reveal her courage and her refusal to be intimidated by wealth or rank, qualities that make her an unusual and captivating character within Austen's world.

Fitzwilliam Darcy: A Man of Pride and Reserve

Fitzwilliam Darcy, often referred to simply as Mr. Darcy, is initially introduced as an aloof and arrogant gentleman. Darcy hails from the landed gentry, with a large estate and significant wealth. His social circle and upbringing have instilled in him a strong sense of pride and a reserved manner. He is unaccustomed to interacting with people outside his social class, and his first impressions of Elizabeth reflect his initial inability to see past these societal distinctions.

However, Darcy's pride is accompanied by a deep sense of responsibility and honor. Despite his initial coldness, he is genuinely kind-hearted and loyal to those he loves. His affection for his sister, Georgiana, and his protective nature are qualities that eventually endear him to Elizabeth as she learns more about his true character.

The Meeting at Meryton and the Dance at Netherfield

The story of Elizabeth and Darcy begins in Meryton, a small town in Hertfordshire, where the Bennet family resides. Mr.

Darcy arrives in the area with his friend Mr. Bingley, who quickly falls in love with Elizabeth's older sister, Jane Bennet. Darcy, however, is less than impressed with the social environment and is overheard dismissing Elizabeth as "tolerable, but not handsome enough to tempt" him. This insult forms Elizabeth's first impression of Darcy as arrogant and haughty, and she responds with a playful disdain for him.

Their paths cross again at a ball at Netherfield, where Darcy's interest in Elizabeth grows. Elizabeth, however, remains uninterested, still holding on to her initial judgment of Darcy's character. These early encounters are marked by tension and misunderstanding, setting the stage for their relationship's evolution.

The Proposal at Hunsford: Clashing Perspectives

One of the most pivotal scenes in *Pride and Prejudice* is Darcy's first proposal to Elizabeth at Hunsford. Darcy confesses his love for her in a manner that is both impassioned and condescending. He acknowledges his social superiority and implies that he is overlooking Elizabeth's lower status because of his affection for her. Instead of winning her over, Darcy's words anger Elizabeth, who accuses him of being arrogant and prejudiced. She also confronts him about his role in separating Jane and Mr. Bingley and accuses him of mistreating Mr. Wickham, a man she believes has been wronged by Darcy.

This confrontation is transformative for both characters. Elizabeth's rejection shocks Darcy and forces him to reflect on his behaviour and attitudes. He realises that his pride has blinded him to his flaws, and he begins to reassess how he interacts with others. For Elizabeth, the proposal serves as a moment of self-reflection as well, especially after she receives a letter from

Darcy explaining his actions regarding Jane and Wickham. She realises that her judgment of Darcy was also influenced by her own prejudices, and she begins to question the assumptions she had made about him.

Darcy's Transformation and Elizabeth's Changing Perception

Following the failed proposal, Darcy undergoes a transformation. Determined to improve himself, he reflects on his flaws and works to become a man worthy of Elizabeth's respect. When Elizabeth later visits Darcy's estate, Pemberley, she sees a different side of him. The accounts of his servants and his warm interactions with his sister reveal a caring, honourable man who is very different from the proud figure she first encountered. Elizabeth's view of Darcy softens, and she starts to see him as someone she could genuinely admire.

In turn, Darcy's reformed behaviour is evident when he learns of Lydia Bennet's scandalous elopement with Mr. Wickham. Recognising the potential damage to the Bennet family's reputation and Elizabeth's distress, Darcy intervenes discreetly. His actions show his selflessness and his willingness to prioritise Elizabeth's happiness over his own pride, even if he receives no recognition or reward.

The Final Proposal: Love and Mutual Respect

In the final chapters, Darcy and Elizabeth's relationship reaches its culmination. Having grown through their misunderstandings and challenges, they come together as equals, with a deep respect and love for one another. Darcy proposes again, this time humbly and with true affection, and Elizabeth accepts. Their marriage symbolises the triumph of genuine connection over superficial concerns like wealth, class, and social expectations.

Their union also reflects Austen's subtle critique of Regency society. Elizabeth and Darcy's love story defies the norms that dictate marriage should be a transaction for financial security or social advantage. Instead, their relationship is based on mutual understanding, personal growth, and a shared sense of values.

Legacy and Cultural Impact

The story of Elizabeth and Darcy has left an indelible mark on literature and popular culture. *Pride and Prejudice* has been adapted countless times in films, television series, and modern retellings. The novel's themes of love, independence, and personal growth continue to resonate with readers worldwide. Elizabeth Bennet and Mr. Darcy have come to symbolise the transformative power of love and self-awareness, and their journey from misunderstanding to harmony has made them icons of romantic literature.

Austen's portrayal of these characters endures because it presents a nuanced exploration of human relationships and personal development. Elizabeth and Darcy are not idealised heroes but flawed, relatable individuals who learn from their mistakes and grow together. In a world where love stories often hinge on simple romance, the tale of Elizabeth and Darcy remains compelling because it delves into the complexities of personality, prejudice, and self-discovery.

Through Elizabeth Bennet and Fitzwilliam Darcy, Austen crafted a love story that goes beyond the superficial, offering readers an enduring lesson on the importance of humility, resilience, and genuine connection. Their journey exemplifies the idea that true love often requires setting aside pride and prejudice in order to fully understand and accept another person, and in so doing, it reveals the best in each partner.

*****

In *Pride and Prejudice,* Mr. George Wickham and Miss Lydia Bennet are characters whose choices and behaviours disrupt the lives of those around them, adding intrigue and drama to Jane Austen's story. Both Wickham and Lydia embody aspects of recklessness, self-interest, and impulsivity, and their actions serve as a counterpoint to the more thoughtful and restrained characters in the novel, like Elizabeth Bennet and Mr. Darcy. Through them, Austen explores themes of deception, vanity, and the consequences of disregarding societal expectations.

George Wickham
The Charming Rogue

Mr. Wickham is a charming but deceitful officer who initially impresses the residents of Meryton with his good looks and engaging manners. Early in the novel, he quickly wins Elizabeth Bennet's sympathy by sharing a story that portrays Mr. Darcy as cruel and unjust. He claims that Darcy denied him a valuable inheritance left by Darcy's father, a tale designed to cast Darcy in a negative light while presenting Wickham as a victim. Wickham's charismatic personality and smooth-talking ways deceive Elizabeth and the Meryton community, who are unaware of his true nature.

In reality, Wickham is morally dubious and financially irresponsible. His charm conceals a man who repeatedly tries to manipulate those around him for his own gain. He has squandered his inheritance through gambling and other poor decisions and seeks financial support through whatever means possible, even attempting to elope with Darcy's younger sister, Georgiana, to gain access to her fortune. This plot was thwarted, and Darcy paid him off to prevent further scandal.

Wickham's motivations are ultimately driven by self-interest and a lack of moral integrity, a stark contrast to Darcy's reserved but deeply ethical character. His deceitful behaviour serves as a catalyst for the development of Elizabeth's understanding of Darcy and helps her to see past her initial prejudices.

Lydia Bennet
The Impulsive Youngest Daughter

Lydia Bennet, the youngest of the Bennet sisters, is characterised by her impulsive and flirtatious personality. Her behaviour is a constant source of embarrassment to her family, particularly her elder sisters, Jane and Elizabeth. Lydia is naïve, attention-seeking, and, like Wickham, unmindful of the consequences of her actions. Her unchecked behaviour reflects the lack of guidance from her mother, Mrs. Bennet, who often encourages Lydia's flirtations without considering the potential fallout.

Lydia's elopement with Wickham shocks the Bennet family and threatens to ruin the reputation of all the Bennet sisters, jeopardising their chances of making respectable marriages. In the context of Regency England, an elopement, especially with a man of questionable character like Wickham, would have been scandalous and could result in social ostracism. Darcy ultimately intervenes to rescue the situation, paying Wickham a significant sum to ensure he marries Lydia, thereby protecting the family's reputation.

Through Lydia and Wickham's relationship, Austen critiques the dangers of unchecked vanity and recklessness, especially in a society where reputation was crucial. Lydia's impulsive behaviour and Wickham's duplicity highlight the consequences of disregarding social norms and underscore the contrast between characters driven by self-interest and those guided by integrity. In the end, while Wickham and Lydia's marriage preserves the Bennet family's honour, it is not based on love or mutual respect, reflecting the precarious nature of relationships formed on shallow or self-serving motivations.

****

Love & Tragedy
At
Pemberley

Did you love *Love & Tragedy At Pemberley*? Then you should read *Elizabeth of Pemberley*[1] by Darryl Martel!

[2]

<u>Elizabeth of Pemberley</u>

After the wedding to the most handsome man, Mr Fitzwilliam Darcy, Elizabeth Bennett, now Mrs Elizabeth Darcy arrives as the new Mistress of Pemberley. With fear, intimidation, but also with excitement, she steps through the door of this great estate. All the servants are lined up and Mrs Reynolds, the Housekeeper, welcomes her Master and her new Mistress home.

---

1. https://books2read.com/u/3GLDKr

2. https://books2read.com/u/3GLDKr

9 798822 774180